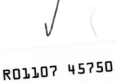

The Jezebel Wolf

F. N. MONJO

The Jezebel
Wolf

illustrated by John Schoenherr

SIMON AND SCHUSTER

NEW YORK

For *Charles and Justin*

Text copyright © 1971 by F. N. Monjo
Illustrations copyright © 1971 by John Schoenherr
Published by Simon and Schuster, Children's Book Division
Rockefeller Center, 630 Fifth Avenue
New York, New York 10020
First Printing

SBN 671-65191-9

Library of Congress Catalog Card Number: 73-144225

Manufactured in the United States of America

Contents

The Gray Wolfskin

"Get over to your side, Danny," said Israel. "You're taking up all the room."

"I am on my side," said Daniel. "You want the whole bed to yourself?"

"You're on my side," said Israel, "and you have all the cover too. Look at you! You have all the quilt and most of the wolfskin too."

Israel sat up in bed. He covered himself with some of the quilt. And he tugged half of the heavy gray wolfskin robe over to his side of the bed.

"This comes from a she-wolf," said Israel, as he pulled it into place.

"Aw, how do you know?" said his brother.

"Pa told me," said Israel, "and I guess he knows. He killed her."

"He never did!" said Daniel, sitting up in surprise. He could see the moon through the frosty window-pane.

"All right. You know so much," said Israel. "Pa *didn't* kill her, then. And you can just go on back to sleep." Israel turned over and buried his head in his pillow.

Daniel stared at the bare wooden floor. A bar of moonlight made a silvery path across the thick warm blanket. He ran his fingers deep into the fur.

"Tell me about it, Israel," he said.

"It was a long time ago," said Israel. "When you were just a baby. You wouldn't remember."

"Tell me about it," said Daniel.

"No, I won't," said Israel. "Just go to sleep."

Daniel punched Israel in the belly.

"Tell me about it," he hollered. "Why can't you tell me, Israel?"

The bedroom door opened, and in came Pa.

"What's all this commotion?" said he. "What's all the fuss?"

"Israel says this fur robe is from a wolf you killed. And I never believed him. And now he won't tell me anything about it," said Daniel.

"Well, I killed her, son, for certain," said Pa.

"Israel Putnam," Ma called, from the next room. "You tell those two boys to go to sleep. And you come get some rest yourself. You'll be waking up baby and the girls before you know it!"

"I'll be there directly, Hannah," said Pa, sitting down at the foot of the bed, on the wolfskin.

"She was a big gray beauty," said Pa. "But she was a killer too. Every farmer here in Pomfret could have told you about her. How she'd killed some of his goats, or a calf, or some sheep. So we swore we'd get her. Back about six, seven years ago. But all that summer and all that fall, she was too smart for the whole lot of us. We couldn't catch her."

"But she was a killer, was she?" said Daniel.

"Huh!" said his brother, sitting up. "She was killing right and left, wasn't she, Pa?"

"Ayeh," said Pa. "I had the nicest little spotted brown-and-white calf you'd ever want to see. That old devil killed her in August. Tore her throat out. Then she chewed up three or four of Increase Durkee's sheep in September. And about a week later, here she come back again and killed two of my nanny goats and three of their little kids. Pretty near every man in Pomfret was hoping to get a shot at her, and had cause for it."

"Tell him about the trap, Pa," said Israel.

" 'Twas a big steel trap," said Pa, nodding grimly. "By the Eternal, I caught her in it, too. But she got away before I'd so much as got a look at her. Trap fastened on three claws of her left front paw. She tore loose and left the three claws behind. Tore herself free!"

"How could she do that?" said Daniel, curling his fingers deep into the gray fur blanket.

"Courage," said Pa. "She gnawed herself loose without a whimper, or I'd have heard her. A wolf will do that, son, plenty of times. So she limped back to her cubs. Got back to her den, wherever that was. None of us farmers 'round about could track her down. Even when we ran her with bloodhounds, we couldn't raise her, nor find her lair. Couldn't even track her in the snow, seemed like. One night in December, she broke into Jabez Williams' sheepfold and killed twelve ewes and three or four lambs.

Blood all over the snow, where the ewes had run out of the fold, throats tore, and blood just pouring out. It was pitiful. The lambs, some of them, bleatin', standin' near their dead mothers, shiverin' in the snow. We must have tracked that wolf thirty miles that night, Jabez and me, 'fore we and the dogs lost her trail at the banks of Muddy Brook. It hadn't iced over, so she run right up it and lost the dogs in the stream. We ran up and down, from Dan to Beer-sheba, trying to pick up her trail, but she give us the slip, clean. We lost her that night, and we kep' on losing her time after time. Each rampage of hers, when she killed stock, we'd go after her. We must have run her thirty, forty times, without no luck at all."

"Israel Putnam," called Ma. "Don't you know it's past ten o'clock? Don't you know it's December? Can't that old chestnut of a story keep till morning? 'Less you come to bed, you'll be down with chills and fever!"

"I'll be there directly, Hannah," said Pa, getting up off the bed.

"Oh, Pa!" said Daniel, "Ain't you going to tell us the rest of the story?"

"It's like enough I will," said Pa, "if so happen you ask for it tomorrow morning." And Pa shut the bedroom door behind him.

Israel and Daniel lay there in the cold bedroom. Moonlight shone on the quiet snowy fields. They heard Pa's bed creak as he settled down beside Ma. Then the boys pulled the big gray wolfskin robe up under their chins and went to sleep.

The Sheepfold

Early next morning, Little Hannah and Elizabeth sat by the hearth in the kitchen, watching Ma cook breakfast. There was a pot of water hanging on a hook over the fire. Baby Mehitabel was in her highchair, staring at the blazing logs. As soon as the water boiled, Ma poured a golden stream of cornmeal into the pot and began stirring up a hasty pudding.

Israel was out back at the shed, bringing in a load of wood for the fire. Daniel was outdoors, too, fetching a bucket of icy water from the well. When Pa came in from the barn, by the covered way, he was carrying two pails of warm milk, steaming in the cold air.

"All the critters are fed," said Pa, "and I could do with some vittles myself."

"Hasty pudding's on the fire," said Ma.

"And hot cider to go with it this cold winter's morning," said Pa. He shoved the poker into the coals on the hearth.

Daniel came in with the water. The bucket thumped on the floor. "Now tell me about the she-wolf, Pa," he said.

"A regular Jezebel she was, in my sights!" said Ma. "And don't seem as if we're ever like to hear the end of her."

"Daniel ain't never heard the story, Ma," said Israel, dropping his load of logs into the wood box by the fire.

"Some of us been hearing it, seems as though, from the first day of Creation," said Ma.

"No reason it can't keep till after breakfast," said Pa.

"Oh, Pa," said Daniel, "what happened after she lamed her paw in the trap? You said you'd tell me, come morning."

"Well, go on, tell the boy, Israel," said Ma.

"If you say so, Hannah," said Pa. "Wolf laid low,

for a month or two," he began. "Then John Sharp, our near neighbor, told me he'd killed two wolf cubs, probably hers, he said. And it seems they must have been hers, as you will hear. For the next night—it must have been early December, right along about this time of year, though hadn't no snow fallen, here come that big gray devil back to our farm. She never made a sound. It was a cold, moonlight night she came. And somehow she broke into the far sheep-fold behind the barn. Murdering mad devil's dam that she was . . . !"

"Israel Putnam!" said Ma. "Keep a tight rein on what you say front of these children."

"Devil's dam she was!" said Pa. "In that one night, Daniel, she killed seventy sheep and goats, right here on this farm alone. We never woke up until she was 'most done with her bloody work. At last we heard the dogs barking, and I ran for my gun. But she was off to the westward, and gone."

"Seventy critters!" said Daniel.

"Oh, Pa!" said Little Hannah. "The poor lambs!"

"She bit and scratched a plenty more that we was able to save," said Pa. "But seventy was dead. Lying stiff and froze in their own blood."

"Hasty pudding's done," said Ma, ladling the cornmeal mush into the bowls on the table. "We might's well have a sup of it while it's hot, 'fore Pa starts tracking that old Jezebel all over the county."

"Well, I was fit to be tied," said Pa. "I swore I'd kill that wolf if it was the last thing I ever did. So I sent Willie out—he was our hired man 'way back then. He rounded up the neighbors—Jabez Williams and Hiram Grant and Increase Durkee, and John and Benoni Sharp—and the seven of us laid our plans."

"Your poker's red hot now, Israel," said Ma.

"So it is," said Pa. And he poured six mugs of cider, and plunged the hot poker into each of them, one by one. Everyone at the table, except Baby Mehitabel, was served some of the warm, frothy drink.

The baby knocked her mug on the table.

"She wants cider, too," said Ma, smiling, as she poured her out another drink of milk.

"What was your plans, Pa?" said Daniel.

"I'm coming to them," said Pa. "All of us got our best bloodhounds together. I chose old Grandsire, my best hound. But you won't remember him, Daniel. He's dead long ago. And Jabez Williams brought his Slasher. And Hiram Grant brought his pair, Jubal and Tubal. And Increase Durkee brought his Spot. And we vowed we'd track that devil down if it took all day and all night and then some."

"And that's just what it did take," said Ma, with a shake of her head. "I never will forget it. We best finish up breakfast real quick, Israel," said Ma. "For I can see it will be near noontime before that she-wolf Jezebel parts with her hide."

The Hunt

Ma was right. Pa's story carried on clear through breakfast. Then Pa told the boys to follow him out back to the barn, where he and Willie, the hired man, were going to shoe Old Red.

"When you shoe an ox big as Old Red is," said Pa, "you must put him in a frame and hoist him up off the ground in a sling. Oxen are too heavy to stand on three feet. They'd topple over."

Willie and Pa eased Old Red up off the barn floor. The ox roared and bellowed in his sling, but his feet were trussed up, so he couldn't kick. Willie squeezed the bellows and sent a stream of air into the fire in the forge, and the charcoal commenced glowing red-hot. Pa rolled up his sleeves and picked up his sledge-hammer. He slammed it down on the anvil with a ringing crash. Sparks jumped out where the hammer struck. Israel wondered if anyone else had arms as big around and strong as Pa's.

"I been telling these boys how we took that she-wolf, Willie. Back in 'forty-two," said Pa.

"She like to run us clear out of Connecticut colony," Willie laughed.

"She did that," said Pa. He grinned at Willie, slammed his hammer down with a clang, and made another big shower of blue sparks jump out of the anvil. "Out we went, the seven of us, with our five bloodhounds, trying to follow that she-wolf's trail. The dogs had her scent. But she was too smart to run for her den. Besides, her cubs were dead by then, anyway, and she only had herself to look out for. She was a crafty devil. But this day, luck turned against her."

"How come, Pa?" said Daniel.

"Well, Dan'l," said Pa, "that old wolf used to throw the dogs off the scent by wading into Still River, or Muddy Brook, and running down the

course of the streams. That way, the dogs couldn't smell out her trail, and they'd lose her. And we couldn't tell where she'd gone. She'd lost us that way every time we trailed her before. And with that same old trick."

"But this time, it was different," said Israel.

"Sure was," said Willie. "This time the hand of Providence reached down and helped us. 'Cause this time, the weather had turned."

"How do you mean?" said Daniel.

"It was December," said Pa. "The ground was hard as this anvil. Stiff with frost. And that old wolf's favorite streams was froze up tight."

"Hey!" said Daniel, his mouth opening in a round O of surprise.

"We knew we was hot on her trail, around ten that morning, because the dogs was yapping with excitement. Then the sky turned gray. Lead color. You know. That cold blue-gray, like a bruise?"

"Ayeh," said Daniel.

"Then it commenced to snow," said Pa. "And me and Jabez Williams and Hiram Grant and Increase Durkee and John and Benoni Sharp and Willie, here, we just hollered, we was so happy."

"Prettiest snow I ever see," said Willie.

"We knew we had her, once we saw that snow," said Pa. "And sure enough, an hour after it began to fall—we was heading west, you see—we run down the bank to cross Natchaug River. And there, on the ice, printed right out, neat as you please in that fresh snow, we come upon her tracks! Tracks of a big wolf, wide spaced, because she was traveling fast. There was three claws missing from the left front paw. It had to be her!"

"That's the paw she caught in the trap," said Israel.

"I know," said Daniel. "I know!"

"We figured she was about a half hour ahead of us, going straight west, heading direct for the Connecticut River. But that river's too wide and too swift to be froze up solid across, so early in winter. And I figured she wouldn't try swimming it, neither. So I hoped maybe we'd bring her to bay when we come up to it."

"Were you gaining on her, Pa?" asked Daniel.

"Hard to tell, with the snow still falling in her tracks. We followed close as we could, hoping for the best, all afternoon long. We crossed five more

frozen streams. Then the snow stopped falling, and the wind come up, and night closed in. But our luck still held. Because the clouds blew over, and the moon come out bright from behind them. And the sky turned starry and clear. So we had plenty of light to follow her trail in the snow."

"Will you take me hunting with you sometime, Pa?" said Daniel.

"Soon's you're able to hit your mark with your rifle, I will," said Pa. "Say, Willie, how's that fire coming?"

"Hot, hot, hot," said Willie. "Hot as the Old Nick. Hot enough to begin."

Pa had been trimming and paring Old Red's cloven hoof. Now he matched the two halves of the cold iron shoe to the ox's hoof. Then he clamped one of the halves of the shoe in a pair of tongs, and thrust it into the red-hot coals in the forge.

"Then what happened, when you come up to Connecticut River, Pa?" said Daniel.

"Well, sir," said Pa, "just as we began drawing near the river, we see the tracks had veered north. The sly old devil had given us the slip, after all. She doubled back on her own trail, too, for soon the tracks was heading back east again, right back toward Pomfret! And here we'd been chasing her due *west* for more than ten hours!"

"All of us sure was downhearted," said Willie.

"I thought maybe we should give it up," said Pa. "We was all tired. My old hound, Grandsire, had ice in his paws, and he was limping. But something in me just wouldn't let go, when I thought of all them sheep she'd killed. And while I was thinkin' about it, pantin' for breath, runnin' along behind the dogs, that's the first time I heard her howl. Ever hear a wolf howl? Low, mournful, and wild. She let loose just once. I reckoned she must be a mile ahead of us, two at most. And Johnny Sharp—he was about seventeen then—he heard it, too, and he said 'Come on, Israel, we can catch her,' and I said, 'By the Eternal, Johnny, let's see if we can't.'

"But when she howled, Grandsire and all the rest of the dogs commenced yappin' and hollerin' like a pack of devils. And I wasn't so simple but I couldn't figger if we could hear her, she had to be able to hear us. So I knowed we'd be in for some hard runnin' before daylight. And a hard run we had, stumpin' 'long through the snow, follerin' that Jezebel eastward."

"You had to run her all night long?" said Daniel. Pa nodded.

"We run back every step of the way we come. The whole thirty-five miles all over again. Crossed every one of them frozen streams we crossed the afternoon before. Sometimes two of us would follow hard on the dogs, and let the rest of the pack and the other boys fall back and rest. Then we'd change off, and two more fellows would come up front and press after her, and give us a chance to fall back and get some rest, by turns. Indians'll do that, you know, when they're running game. But sometimes even the men and the dogs in the lead had to flop down in the snow for a breather. And whenever that happened I 'magine that old Jezebel had some way of knowin' it, and set herself down for a rest, too. I say I *'magine* that's what she done, 'cause none of us clapped eyes on her, all night long! We was mighty tired, I can tell you, when we tramped back into Pomfret township next morning at six o'clock. The sun was comin' up red. And the snow on the hemlocks had turned pink in the light of dawn . . ."

The Wolf Den

Old Red, the ox, let out a bellow when Pa began nailing the shoe onto his hoof.

"By the Eternal," Daniel hollered, "he scared me sure enough. I thought 'twas the old wolf howling, just for a minute there."

Pa and Willie laughed.

"We be done with Old Red in another few minutes," said Pa. "The one half's nailed on tight. And the other half will be hot enough to shape before you know it."

Old Red bellowed again from his sling. This time Daniel and Israel laughed, too, right along with the men.

30

"Well, sir," said Pa, " 'twas Johnny Sharp found out where the old wolf's den was at. He was younger than all the rest of us, and running so hard on her trail that he had her in sight soon after sunup. And she was mighty tired after her seventy-mile run that night. Same as all the rest of us who'd been trailing her. And don't you know that that devil's dam had made her den in a jumble of granite boulders on a hillside, not three miles from my own farm? Isn't that a fact, Willie?"

"That's right, Mr. Israel," said Willie. "Right over on that hillside 'bout a mile from Sharp's homestead."

"Soon's we'd seen where her den was," said Pa, "the dogs run up and started hollerin' around the entrance. We built a fire just inside, hoping to smoke her out. But it didn't seem to bother her none. Least she never made a move to come out."

"Then Benoni Sharp and me went over to his place to fetch some more men and guns, and to get us some sulphur to put on the fire. Sulphur makes a real thick smoke, and a horrible smell," said Willie.

"And when they come back, we tried burning some right inside the mouth of the den, but she just wasn't going to be smoked out. So we tried to send Grandsire in after her, and we heard a fearful growlin' and shrieking. And Grandsire come wrigglin' out with his jowls all bloody and his ear tore. Nothing we could do would make that hound go back inside. Then Jabez Williams sent in his big Slasher. And there was more snapping and growling and screeching. Then out come Slasher, limpin' and bleedin', and *he* wouldn't go back in there neither! None of the rest of the dogs would even attempt it, after they seen what happened to Grandsire and Slasher."

"Then your Pa went in after her himself," said Willie.

"Pa! You never did!" said Daniel.

"I told you Pa killed her," said Israel. "Didn't I *tell* you?"

"You never told me he followed her right into her den!" said Daniel.

"I swore she wasn't going to kill one more lamb belonged to Israel Putnam," said Pa. "So I pulled off my coat and my waistcoat, and I went over to a birch tree and stripped off some bark, and twisted the strips together to make a kind of torch. And I told Jabez

Williams and Hiram Grant and Increase Durkee and Johnny Sharp to tie a good long rope to my feet, and to pull me back out, real quick, when I signaled. I was going to kick my legs, and pull hard on the rope, you see. Then I loaded my gun with buckshot. And I lit my birchbark torch. And I got down on my belly in the snow. And I started crawling into that cave."

"Other half of Old Red's shoe is ready, Mr. Israel," said Willie, pointing to the forge.

"So it is," said Pa, plucking it out with the tongs and laying it on the anvil. "I'll just knock it into shape, and then we'll be done."

Pa's hammer slammed down, clang after clang after clang. After every slam, a shower of white-hot sparks danced on the anvil and sprayed up into the air.

"Come on, Pa," said Daniel. "You was just crawling into the cave."

"That's right, I was," said Pa, with a grin at Daniel. "And you know what I found in that den? It sloped down from the entrance. For about fifteen feet it just kept on going down, down, the whole way. Floor was slippery as glass, too, on account of

water had seeped onto it from the rocks, and then froze to solid ice. After I'd slid down that first fifteen feet, the floor finally leveled off. And the level place run back about another ten feet. And here I was with that flickering torch in one hand, and my gun in the other, so I couldn't even crawl very fast. Cold and damp, and only about two feet of space from floor to ceiling. But the birchbark torch didn't go out, thank the Eternal, and I kept on crawling. Now, by this time I'm about twenty-five feet from the entrance, inside that den, when the passage starts climbing gradually. So I hold up my smoking torch, and about sixteen feet ahead of me I see two big orange eyes gleaming at me. It's the wolf, and she's growling and snapping and moaning. And rubbing her head between her two front paws."

Pa clanged his hammer down on the anvil, and there was a hiss and a cloud of steam when he dropped the red-hot shoe into a bucket of water. Daniel jumped as if he'd been shot, and everybody laughed.

Pa fished the shoe out of the bucket and nailed it onto Old Red's hoof. Then he and Willie untied his other three feet, and lowered the ox, snorting

and bellowing, back down onto the barn floor. Willie slipped the sling out from under him, and led him back into his stall.

"That's done," said Pa, thumping the hammer down beside the anvil. He took one look at Daniel and went back to his story. "Well, the wolf snarled," said Pa, "and I was so surprised I kicked my feet hard. And Jabez and Hiram and Increase and Johnny Sharp hauled me out of the den, backwards, so fast I dropped my torch. My shirt was pulled right off my back. My chest and my face was all scratched up on that icy floor. I come floundering out onto the snow. I was mad as a hornet. 'What did you do that for, you numbskulls?' I hollered. Called them dunces and boobies, too. I was thundering mad."

"That's right, Daniel," said Willie. "You never see your Pa so mad as he was when we pulled him out of that cave."

"So I made me another birchbark torch, grabbed my gun, and crawled back in a second time," said Pa.

"And we was all hollerin' 'Don't go back in. Don't go back in!'" said Willie.

"I crawled down the slope, across the level space,

and started up the rise. That she-devil is still there. Madder than ever. Growling. Snapping her teeth. Just as she's ready to spring at me, I aim right between her eyes. The gun goes off with a roar and a cloud of smoke fills the den. I start coughing. The boys commence hauling me out again, backwards. And there I am for the second time, lying outside in the snow."

"Was she dead, Pa?" said Daniel. "Had you killed her?"

"How was Pa to know?" said Israel.

"Didn't nobody know if she was dead," said Willie.

"We couldn't hear a sound from inside," said Pa. "But the dogs kept yapping and barking, all excited, so I couldn't be sure. So I loaded my gun, lit the torch again, and started in a third time. Going slow and cautious. Down the slope, across the level place, and then up the rise. There she lay in the dark, still as a stone, her head between her paws. I reached out with my torch. Still she didn't move. I even touched it against her nose. She never stirred so much as a quiver. She was dead. So I grabbed her hard, by the ears, and kicked my feet. The boys started heaving and pulling on the rope. And here I come up out of the den and into the snow, for the third and last time. Only this time I'm being pulled backwards on my belly. And I'm dragging that she-devil behind me. Heavy as she can be. Limp, and silent, and dead as a doornail."

The Jubilee

"I was tolerable pleased," said Pa, "when I saw 'twas all over and I was safe out of that icy cave."

"All of us was hollerin' and stompin' and yellin'," said Willie.

"By that time half the countryside had heard we'd trapped the she-wolf in her lair, and there was a parcel of neighbors standin' around in the snow, outside the den, waitin' to hear all about it," said Pa. "Nearest house was over to Sharp's farm," he continued, "and Johnny and Benoni said we must every one of us troop over to their place for an uproarious, whoopin' jubilee, on account of killin' that

sheep-murderin' Jezebel at last. So we drag her car-
cass through the snow, and all of us stepped over
to the Sharps' place."

"It was gettin' late in the day, then," said Willie.

"Ayeh," said Pa. "The sun had begun to set.
Sleighs full of neighbors come jinglin' into the barnyard, as the news traveled. Folks from miles around
rode over to have a look at the she-wolf that'd been
slaughterin' their calves and lambs longer'n any-
body cared to remember."

"How big was she, Pa?" said Israel.

"More'n five feet long. Big powerful brute. We
hung her up, on a beam, high's we could, on the
outside of the barn, so's everybody could get a good
look at her, before I skinned her hide. And Increase
Durkee went home to fetch a keg of rum. I come
over home to fetch a barrel of hard cider. Jabez
Williams and Hiram Grant and Benoni Sharp built
a big bonfire in the snow in the Sharps' barnyard.
I must have told my story to the whole township,
pretty near, and the men drunk three monstrous big
toasts, one for each time I'd crawled into that gray
wolf's den. And then somebody—maybe it was you,
Willie—commenced fiddlin' and before you could

say Jehoshaphat, half of Pomfret township come crowdin' onto Benoni Sharp's threshin' floor. There was laughin' and jostlin' and jiggin' and dancin' and drinkin' till well past midnight. Then the bonfire burned down to a ring of cracklin' sparks. And we all agreed that the she-wolf had give us all the excuse we needed to have us a thunderin' Yankee-good romp. Then we all started off for home in the frosty night, stars shinin' overhead, and my head so turned 'round by all that toastin' that I clean forgot till next morning that I'd never yet took her hide. . . ."

Ma came to the kitchen door, smiling. She asked Pa had he killed off that Jezebel she-wolf yet. Pa walked back to the house, telling her yes, he had. Willie went off to the sheepfold, to do some chores amongst the lambs. And after lunch Israel and Daniel took Little Hannah down to the brook, and spent the afternoon sliding on the ice.

That night, when the two boys were lying in bed, in their room, waiting for sleep to come, Daniel said, "Israel, you calculate there's any more wolves like that around Pomfret?"

"Aw, Daniel," said Israel, "how do I know?

What's the matter? Pa scare you with that story?"

"No," said Daniel, pulling the wolfskin robe up against his cheek. "He didn't scare me none."

"Then get over on your side of the bed, and let me have some cover," said Israel. "And go to sleep."

"I *am* on my side," said Daniel.

"And don't be scared, now, hear?" said Israel. "If any more timberwolves come around here, Pa'll catch 'em."

"Sure he will," said Daniel. "Same as he caught this one." He ran his fingers deep into the soft, heavy fur. He imagined he could hear a wolf howling, away off in the woods that lay beyond the fields. He listened harder, but everything was still. A bar of moonlight fell across the floor and over the thick gray wolfskin. He buried his head in his pillow, in case the wolf should howl again.

"Pa could catch him sure," he murmured. "If there *was* a wolf, I mean."

About this Story

In writing this story, I invented the name of Israel Putnam's hired hand, the names of most of his neighbors, and the names of the dogs who took part in his famous wolf hunt. The rest of the facts are based on a story Putnam himself told, many times over, during his long, adventurous life.

In the French and Indian War, Israel Putnam (1718–1790) was a captain in Major Robert Rogers' remarkable band of rangers, who fought at Lake George and around Fort Ticonderoga on Lake Champlain. Putnam was captured by Indians, taken to Canada as a prisoner, and later ransomed. Twenty

years later, during the American Revolution, Major-
General Israel Putnam was one of George Washing-
ton's doughtiest officers in the Continental Army.
At the Battle of Bunker Hill, it was "Old Put" who
told his soldiers not to fire at the redcoats "till you
see the whites of their eyes." (And, incidentally, he
also wrote some of the most downright and glori-
ously misspelled letters I've ever had the good for-
tune to read.)

At the time this wolf hunt took place, Putnam
had not yet become a famous man. It occurred in the
winter of 1742–43, many years before his soldiering
began, when he was a young farmer, about twenty-
five years old.

Putnam's wolf den is up in Pomfret, Connecticut,
and may still be seen today.

A final word about the she-wolf herself. In these
days when so much of our wildlife is in danger, I
should be sorry if readers of this story were to con-
clude that I must be an enemy of wolves, and must
wish to see their species exterminated. For that is not
so: I hope we will pass laws so that wolves can
survive, somehow, along with the moose and the
buffalo, the sea otter, the peregrine falcon, the mus-

tang, and thousands of other animals now threat-
ened with extinction. But in reading stories dealing
with the past, readers must remember that attitudes
and feelings change with changed circumstances,
over the centuries, just as do customs and costumes,
and that wolves were numerous enough in New
England, two hundred years ago, to be universally
dreaded and hated; which is to say, that, had we
lived in Pomfret, Connecticut, in the 1740's when
wolves were far from being in any danger of extermi-
nation, we would almost certainly have celebrated
with Israel Putnam, when the great gray wolf was
killed.

My principal reasons for retelling a tale which
Putnam liked to repeat, and which was popular a
century ago with schoolchildren, are brief. I think it
is a gripping story in its own right and one which
embodies an act of frontier courage that backward-
looking addicts of nostalgia (such as I) would like
to believe to be distinctively American.